For Ella and Ben

A special thanks to Josh, Julie, and Alan

www.mascotbooks.com

ALL TIED UP

©2020 Gina Moulton. All Rights Reserved. No part of this publication may be reproduced, stored in a retrieval system or transmitted in any form by any means electronic, mechanical, or photocopying, recording or otherwise without the permission of the author.

For more information, please contact:
Mascot Books
620 Herndon Parkway, Suite 320
Herndon, VA 20170
info@mascotbooks.com

Library of Congress Control Number: 2020901259

CPSIA Code: PRT0120
ISBN-13: 978-1-64307-423-8

Printed in the United States

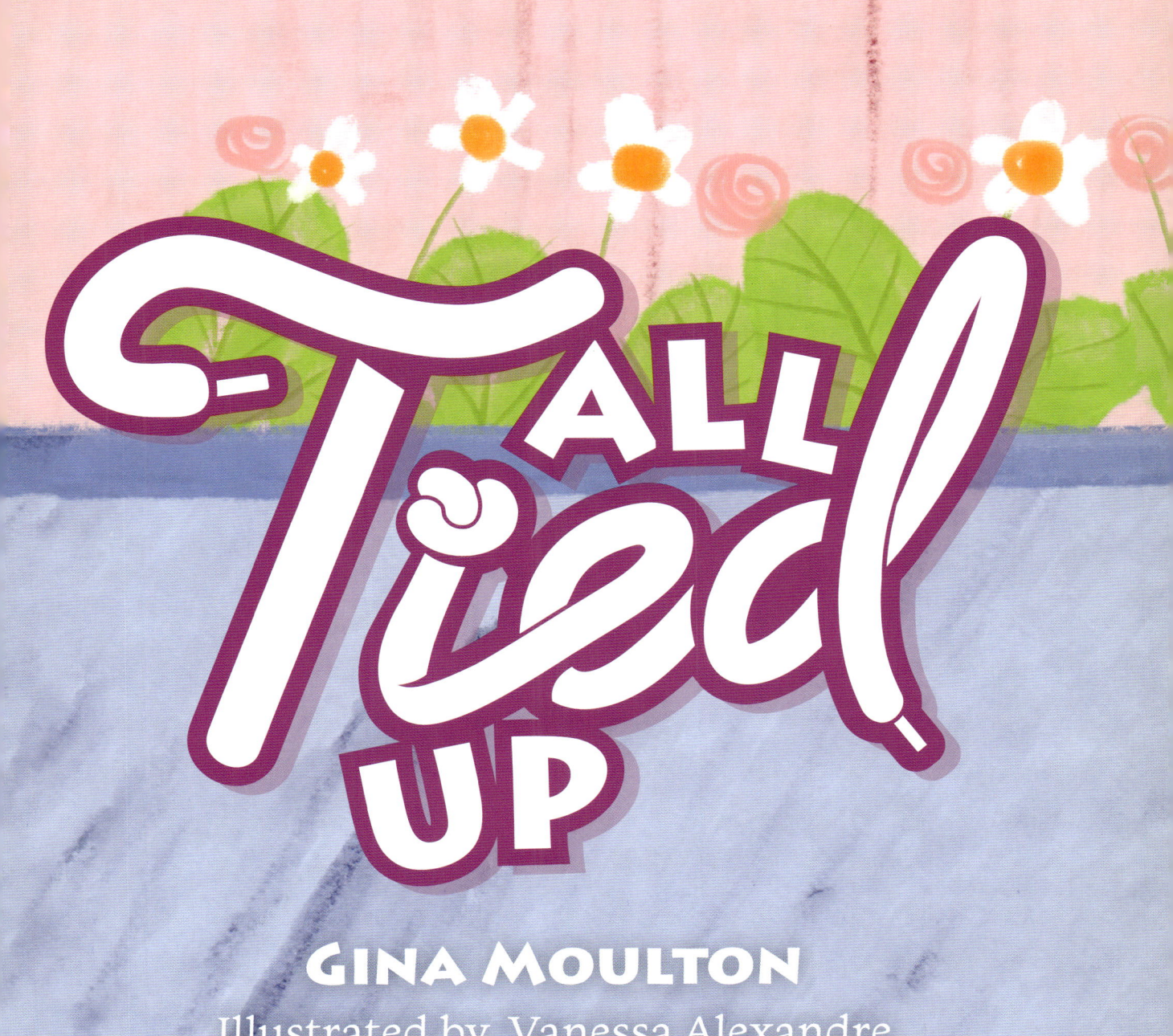

All Tied Up

Gina Moulton

Illustrated by Vanessa Alexandre

This is Ella. She is five-and-a-half years old and loves kindergarten. Ella gets excited to go to school each morning and play with her friends. She loves her teacher, Ms. M, and she also loves reading and counting to one hundred.

But there was one thing Ella did *not* love, in fact, she didn't even *like* it. Not even a little bit. Ella *despised* her class's latest project. Ms. M had challenged all of the children in her class to learn how to tie their own shoes.

Ms. M told the class, "If you practice tying your shoes for the rest of the school year, you can earn a prize from the prize box." Ms. M had a *great* prize box. It was filled with really cool things like strawberry-shaped erasers (that really smelled like strawberries), tiny dinosaurs that grew into large dinosaurs, notebooks, and squishy toy frogs. Ella really wanted to earn the green squishy frog that could stretch and soar through the air like a rubber band.

Ms. M explained, "There is a prize in the box for each of you. Everyone who really tries and makes an effort to learn will earn a prize by the end of the school year. You will even earn a prize if you haven't learned how to tie your shoes yet. The prize is for *trying* to tie your shoes. Some children learn how to tie their shoes in preschool, some in kindergarten, and some when they are older."

"We all learn how to do things at different times," Ms. M continued. "The important thing to remember is to never give up. Take the time to practice each night and ask an adult or a friend for help if you need it. Most importantly, keep trying even when you make a mistake. After all, we can learn from our mistakes!" said Ms. M. excitedly. "Remember friends, if you want to learn something new, it will take a lot of effort!"

Julie raised her hand and asked, "What is effort?"

Ms. M explained, "Effort is taking the time to do something or practice something, even when it is hard to do, and not giving up when it seems too hard or when you make mistakes. It is important to have lots of strategies or ways to do something so that when you make a mistake, you can try again a different way."

Over the next few days, Ms. M showed her students how to tie their shoes. First, she demonstrated how to make an X and tuck one lace under the other. She reminded them to pull the laces tight before beginning the next part. Ella watched as her friends Tovah and Gia learned how to tie their shoes. Tovah told Ella that she practiced with her older brother every night.

Ella decided to try to tie her shoes but her very first time, she tied her finger up into her laces! "Oh, no!" cried Ella. The second time, Ella tied her laces together into a gigantic knot. She felt embarrassed and wanted to hide.

Ella's stomach felt like it was all tied up in the same gigantic knot as her shoe laces. She decided she must not be as smart as her friends, Tovah and Gia, since they figured out how to tie their shoes and she hadn't. This feeling made Ella want to cry.

Each day, Ella watched as more and more friends learned how to tie their shoes. One day, a boy named James raised his hand and said, "Ms. M! Ms. M! I've been practicing every morning at the bus stop, and I want to show you how I tie my shoes!"

Ms. M watched as he made an x with the laces, tucked one lace under the other, and pulled it tight. Then he made a bunny ear, ran the other lace around the bunny ear through the rabbit hole, making another bunny ear. At the end, he pinched both ears, and James had tied his shoe!

That night, Ella's stomach was all tied up in knots once again. Her mom noticed that Ella seemed worried and asked, "What's wrong, honey?"

Ella replied, "I just don't feel as smart as the other kids in my class because so many of them have figured out how to tie their shoes and I still have no idea how."

Ella's mom listened patiently before giving Ella a smile. "Knowing how to tie your shoes is something you learn to do with practice and good strategies. You will learn how to tie your shoes. You just don't know how to do it yet."

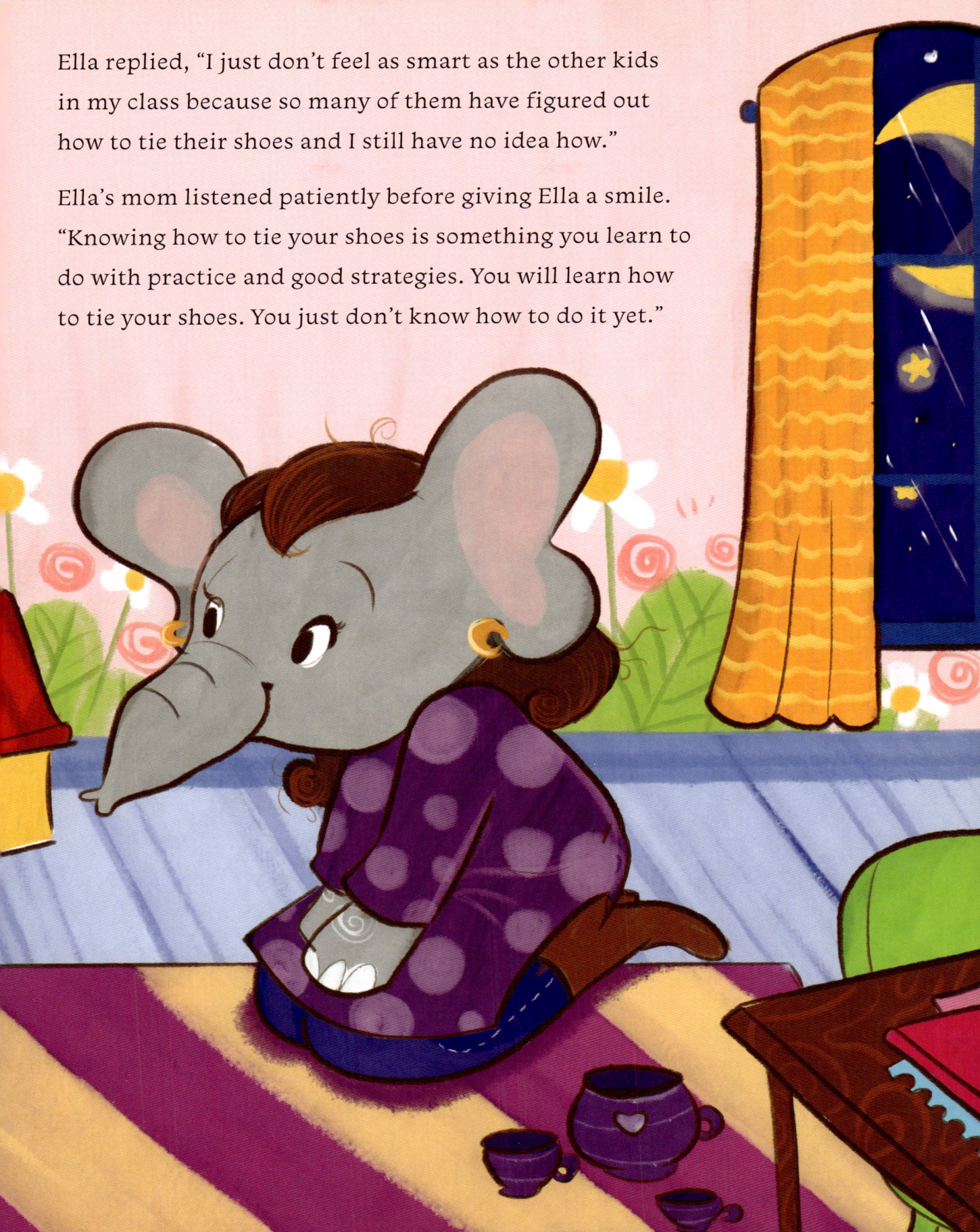

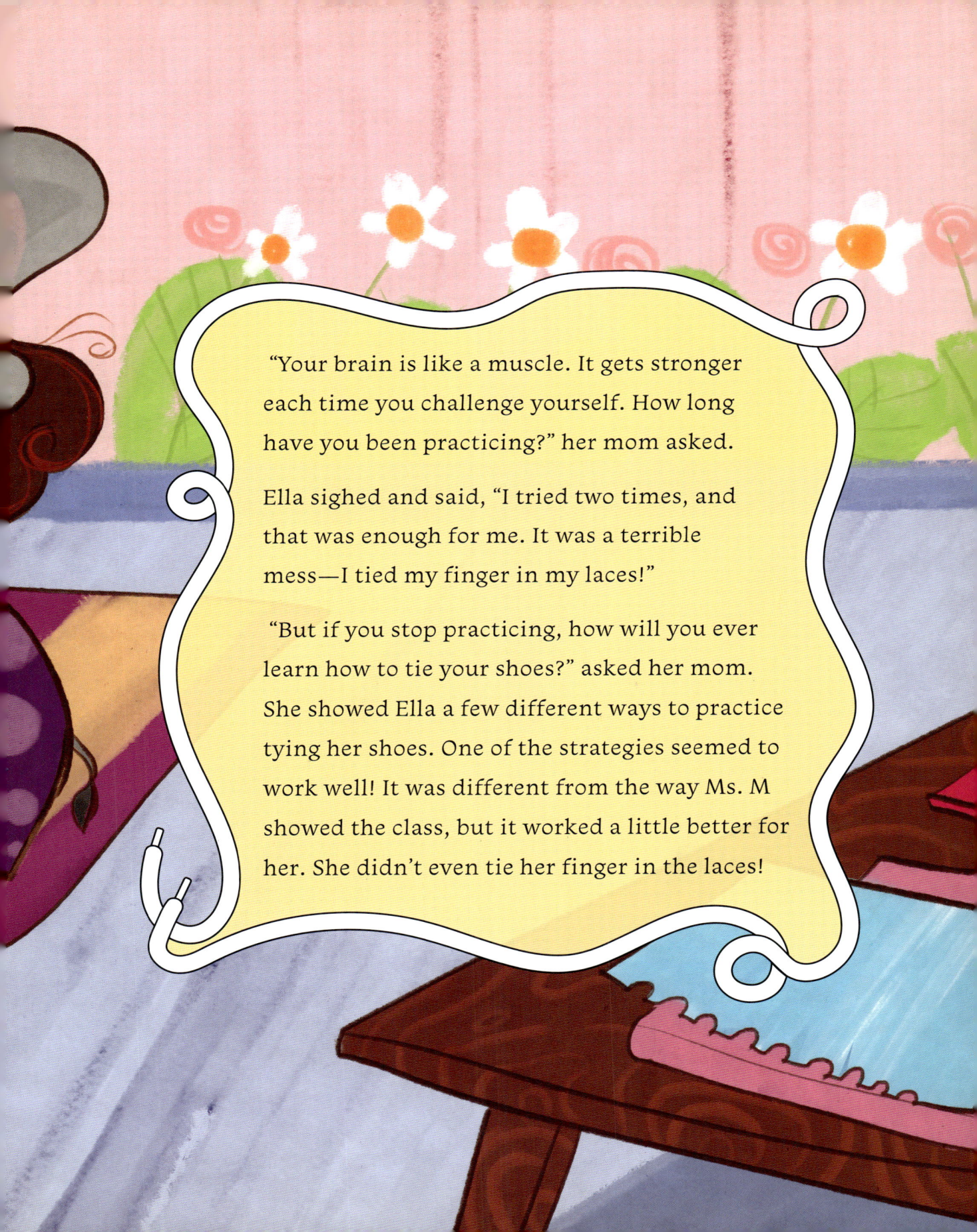

"Your brain is like a muscle. It gets stronger each time you challenge yourself. How long have you been practicing?" her mom asked.

Ella sighed and said, "I tried two times, and that was enough for me. It was a terrible mess—I tied my finger in my laces!"

"But if you stop practicing, how will you ever learn how to tie your shoes?" asked her mom. She showed Ella a few different ways to practice tying her shoes. One of the strategies seemed to work well! It was different from the way Ms. M showed the class, but it worked a little better for her. She didn't even tie her finger in the laces!

Ella worked hard on tying her shoes each day after school. *Is it starting to get a little easier?* she wondered. Maybe it was, but she still could not do it completely.

When her mom walked into Ella's room after dinner, Ella shouted, "I still can't tie my shoes! I have been trying so hard! It's not fair!"

Mom corrected Ella, "You cannot tie your shoes yet, but I believe in you and know you can do it. Keep practicing, my love."

A whole month later, Ella was helping her little brother, Ben, get ready for preschool. After she found Ben's coat and helped him put it on, Ben asked Ella if she would tie his shoes. He even said please! Without thinking, Ella quickly bent down and made a loose bow with the laces. She did it. She tied his laces!

Both Ella's mom and Ben cheered for her! Ella felt proud. Ella, her mom, and Ben were smiling as they left together for school. Ella could not wait to get there and show Ms. M what she learned to do.

When Ella got to school, she tied her shoes beautifully for everyone to see. Ella told her friends, "It wasn't easy, and it took a long time. I tried out a few different strategies and made some mistakes, but I didn't give up. I did it! I learned something new!"

Let's Turn and Talk

- Have you ever felt the way Ella felt?
- How can you learn from your mistakes?
- Why is the word "yet" so special?
- How can your brain become stronger?
- Who can you ask for help when you feel stuck on something?
- What do you want to learn to do?

About the Author

Gina Moulton graduated from the University of Massachusetts Amherst with a Bachelor of Arts in Spanish and a Master's degree in Early Childhood Education. She has taught kindergarten for over fifteen years and continues to be inspired by the confidence many of her young students have in their own abilities to grow and learn new things. For many children, unfortunately, this *growth mindset* shifts to more of a fixed mindset as they get older. To combat this trend, Gina encourages her students to focus on progress and see failures as opportunities to learn.

When she is not teaching kindergarten, Gina enjoys surfing in Mexico and developing her own growth mindset. She currently resides in Western Massachusetts with her husband, two young children, and two old cats.

All Tied Up is Gina's first children's book.